Chiharu's Magic Toothbrush

千春の
魔法の歯ブラシ

Chiharu no mahō no haburashi

Written by Joana Jehu-Appiah

Translated by Kana Sato

Illustrated by Elif Esen Gökçe

and Naya Kirichenko

CHIHARU'S MAGIC TOOTHBRUSH

DEDICATIONS

This book is dedicated to my parents, sisters, and friends.

この本は私の両親、姉妹、そして友人に捧げられています。

Kono hon wa watashi no ryōshin, shimai, soshite yūjin ni sasage rarete imasu。

I am so very grateful to the people that I met in Japan. I will forever treasure the memories.

日本で出会った人々にとても感謝しています。

私はこの思い出を永遠に大切にします。

Nihon de deatta hitobito ni totemo kansha shite imasu. Watashi wa kono omoide o eien ni taisetsu ni shimasu.

Thank you 2020 – For the hard lessons and many blessings.

ありがとう2020年一辛い教えと恩恵の一年でした。学んだ教訓に感謝しています。

Arigatō 2020 - Tsurai oshie to onkei no ichinen deshita. Mananda kyōkun ni kansha shite imasu.

CONTENTS

Used interchangeably

Mother   (okaasan)

Father   (otoosan)

Grandfather   (ojiisan)

Grandmother   (obaasan)

Hotsprings   (onsen)

CHAPTER 1

A Welcomed Gift

ウェルカムギフト

'This is for you.' Yoko handed her daughter a small box.

「これはあなたの物よ。」
陽子は娘に小さな箱を手渡しました。
'Kore wa anata no monoyo.' Yōko wa musume ni chīsana hako o tewatashimashita.

It was beautifully decorated with a ribbon on it.

それはリボンで美しく飾られていました。
Sore wa ribon de utsukushiku kazararete imashita.

'I bought it at work.'

「仕事場で買ったのよ」
'Shigotoba de katta no yo.'

Chiharu took the box and tore off the wrapping excitedly.

千春は箱を取り、興奮して包装をはがしました。
Chiharu wa hako o tori, kōfun shite hōsō o hagashimashita.

'Okaasan!' she cried. 'I love it.' She put it on.

「お母さん！」千春は叫びました。

とてもかわいい！」千春はそれを手首につけました。

'Okāsan!' Chiharu wa sakebimashita.

'Totemo kawaī!' Chiharu wa sore o tekubi ni tsukemashita.

She marvelled at the yellow watch. She promised to look after it.

千春は黄色い腕時計に驚きました。そしてそれを
大切にすることを約束しました。

Chiharu wa kiiroi udedokei ni odoroki mashita. Soshite sore o taisetsu ni suru koto o yakusoku shimashita.

Yoko was happy to see a smile back on her face.

陽子は千春の笑顔を見て嬉しく思いました。

Yōko wa Chiharu no egao o mite ureshiku omoi mashita.

She reached into another shopping bag and brought out some more items.

陽子は別の買い物袋に手を伸ばして、ほかにも買ってきたものを取り出しました。

Yōko wa betsu no kaimonobukuro ni te o nobashite, hoka ni mo katte kita mono o toridashimashita.

'Who are these tools for?' Chiharu asked.

「この道具は誰のためのもの？」と千春は尋ねました。

'Kono dōgu wa dare no tame no mono?' to Chiharu wa tazunemashita.

'Obaachan,' Yoko replied.

「おばあちゃんよ」とヨーコは答えました。

'Obāchan yo.' to Yōko wa kotaemashita.

Once a year, Chiharu and her mother Yoko visit Obaasan in Tokushima, to celebrate Obon (ancestor's remembrance festival).

年に一度、千春とお母さんは徳島のおばあさんを訪ね、お盆を祝います。

Nen ni ichido, Chiharu to Okāsan wa Tokushima no obāsan o tazune, obon o iwai masu.

Tokushima is best known for Awa-Odori (a four-day dance festival) that takes place during Obon. Dance groups, known as ren, practice every day for Awa-Odori.

徳島は、お盆の時期に行われる阿波おどりで有名です。連と呼ばれる踊りのグループは、阿波おどりのために毎日練習しています。

Tokushima wa, obon no jiki ni okonawareru Awa odori de yūmeidesu.
Ren to yobareru odori no gurūpu wa, Awa odori no tame ni mainichi renshū shite imasu.

They chant:
'A yatto sa a Yatto yatto'

阿波踊りのかけ声は：

'ア　ヤットサー、ア　ヤットヤット'

Awa odori no kakegoe wa: 'A yattosā, a yatto yatto'

The thought of Awa Odori made Yoko smile. It

reminded her of her childhood. Chiharu however, was

not so happy this Obon because of a wobbly tooth.

阿波おどりへの想いが陽子を笑顔にさせました。そ
れは陽子の子供時代を思い出させます。
しかし、千春は歯がグラグラするために、このお盆
はそれほど幸せではありませんでした。

Awa odori eno omoi ga Yōko o egao ni sasemashita.
Sore wa Yōko no kodomo jidai o omoidasasemasu. Shikashi, Chiharu wa ha ga
guragurasuru tameni, kono obon wa sorehodo shiawasedewa arimasendeshita.

CHAPTER 2

An Unexpected Gift

思いがけない贈り物

The sun poured through the window and woke Chiharu. It was the day before Obon.

窓から差し込む太陽の光で、千春の目が覚めました。お盆の前日でした。

Mado kara sashikomu taiyō no hikaride Chiharu no me ga samemashita. Obon no zenjitsudeshita.

Chiharu blew a kiss in the air for her late father and grandfather.

千春は亡くなったお父さんとおじいさんに投げキッスをしました。

Chiharu wa nakunatta otōsan to ojīsan ni nage kissu o shimashita.

She stretched her arms and legs and swept past a small object under her pillow. It fell on the floor.

千春が腕と脚を伸ばすと、枕の下の小さな物に触れ、それは床に落ちました。

Chiharu ga ude to ashi o nobasuto, makura no shita no chīsana mono ni fure, sore wa yuka ni ochimashita.

'Chiharu!' Yoko called from the kitchen. 'Breakfast is ready!'

「千春！」陽子は台所から呼びました。

「朝食ができたわよ！」

`Chiharu!' Yōko wa daidokoro kara yobimashita.
`Chōshoku ga dekita wa yo!'

Chiharu got up to go to the bathroom.

千春は起き上がってトイレに行きました。

Chiharu wa okiagatte toire ni ikimashita.

On the way, she stepped on the small object by her bed.

千春はベッドの近くの小さな物を踏んづけました。
Chiharu wa beddo no chikaku no chīsana mono o funzukemashita.

She sighed.

千春はため息をつきました。
Chiharu wa tameiki o tsukimashita.

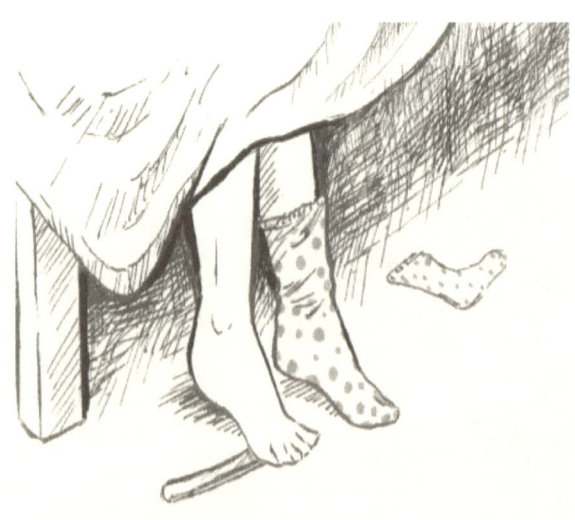

Chiharu dragged a stool to the sink and took a step up.

千春は踏み台を洗面台の前に引っぱってきて乗りました。

Chiharu wa fumidai o senmendai no mae ni hippatte kite norimashita.

As she opened her mouth to brush she was startled.

ちはるは口を開けてはみがきをしようとした時、驚きました。

Chiharu wa kuchi o akete hamigaki o shiyōtoshita toki, odorokimashita.

She dropped her toothbrush in the sink and returned to her bedroom.

千春は歯ブラシをシンクに落とし、寝室に戻りました。

Chiharu wa haburashi o shinkui ni otoshi, shinshitsu ni modori mashita.

Where is it? She wondered.

どこにあるの？　千春は不思議に思いました。

Doko ni aruno? Chiharu wa fushigi ni omoimashita.

'Haru-chan!' Yoko called again. Chiharu picked up the object and made her way to the kitchen.

「はるちゃん！」陽子がまた呼びました。千春はそれを手に取り、台所に向かいました。

`Haru-chan!' Yōko wa mata yobi mashita. Chiharu wa sore o te ni totte daidokoro ni mukaimashita.

'Okaasan, my tooth,' she cried.

「お母さん、私の歯」と千春は叫びました。

`Okāsan, watashi no ha.' to Chiharu wa sakebimashita

'What about your tooth?'

「あなたの歯がどうしたの？」

`Anata no ha ga dō shita no?'

'It's gone.'

「なくなっちゃったの」

`Nakunatchatta no.'

Yoko inspected Chiharu's mouth.

陽子は千春の口を見ました。

Yōko wa Chiharu no kuchi o mimashita.

Yoko told Chiharu that it was perfectly normal for baby teeth to fall out and that it will grow back.

陽子は、子供の歯が抜けるのは普通で、新しい歯が
また生えてくるのよと千春に言いました。

Yōko wa Chiharu ni, kodomo no ha ga nukeruno wa futū de, atarashii ha ga mata haetekurunoyo to Chiharu ni iimashita.

This made Chiharu feel a little better.

この言葉で千春は少し気分が良くなりました。

Kono kotoba de Chiharu wa sukoshi kibun ga yoku narimashita.

Yoko then realised that she would have to break with childhood tradition.

陽子は子供の頃の伝統を破らなければならないことに気づきました。

Yōko wa kodomo no koro no dentō o yaburanakereba naranai koto ni kizukimashita.

'Sadly, I cannot throw your tooth under the floorboards.'

「残念だけど、あなたの歯を床下に投げることはできないの」

'Zannen dakedo, anata no ha o yukashita ni nageru koto wa dekinaino.'

Chiharu frowned and folded her arms.

千春は眉をひそめ、腕を組みました。

Chiharu wa mayu o hisome, ude o kumimashita.

Yoko noticed the small object in her hand.

陽子は千春が手に小さな何かを持っていることに気づきました。

Yōko wa Chiharu ga te ni chīsana nanika o motte iru koto ni kizukimashita.

'What's that?' She asked.

「それは何？」　陽子は尋ねました。

'Sore wa nani?' Yōko wa tazunemashita.

Chiharu revealed the object. Yoko gasped and took off her apron.

千春は陽子にそれを見せました。
陽子は息をのみ、エプロンを脱ぎました。

Chiharu wa Yōko ni sore o misemashita.
Yōko wa iki o nomi, epuron o nugimashita.

She went to the drawer, and took out a pair of chopsticks.

陽子は引き出しに行って箸を取り出し、テーブル
に置きました。

Yōko wa hikidashi ni itte hashi o toridashi, tēburu ni okimashita.

Yoko set the table in a hurry. Chiharu looked at the table. This is not how you set a table she thought. She looked at Yoko questioningly.

陽子は急いで食事の準備をしました。

千春はテーブルを見ました。食器の位置が正しくないなと千春は思い、陽子を不思議そうに見ました。

Yōko wa isoide shokuji no junbi o shimashita.
Chiharu wa tēburu o mimashita. Shokki no ichi ga tadashikunainato Chiharu wa omoi, Yōko o fushigisō ni mimashita.

'The food will get cold.... Itadakimasu.'

'Itadakimasu,' replied Chiharu. They ate.

「食べ物が冷たくなるわ。いただきます」

「いただきます」と千春が答え、食べ始めました。

`Tabemono ga tsumetaku naru wa. Itadakimasu.'
`Itadakimasu.' to Chiharu ga kotae, tabe hajimemashita.

Chiharu stared at the object.

千春はその物体を見つめました。

Chiharu wa sono buttai o mitsumemashita.

It was a toothbrush. It was hard to get excited about a plain wooden toothbrush. Yoko told Chiharu that it was a blessing from the spirits of the past.

それは歯ブラシでした。無地の木製のただの歯ブラ
シに興奮するのは難しいと感じました。

陽子は千春に、それは過去の精霊からの祝福だと語
りました。

Sore wa haburashideshita. Muji no mokusei no tada no haburashi ni kōfun suru no wa muzukashiito kanjimashita. Yōko wa Chiharu ni, sore wa kako no seirei kara no shukufukuda to katarimashita.

Chiharu did not understand.

千春は理解できませんでした。

Chiharu wa rikai dekimasen deshita.

She thought the best place for it would be in the bathroom cabinet.

千春はそれを浴室のキャビネットに保管するのが最適だと思いました。

Chiharu wa sore o yokushitu no kyabinetto ni hokan suruno ga saitekida to omoimashita.

She hopped of her chair and headed for the kitchen door.

千春は椅子からとび下り、台所のドアに向かいました。

Chiharu wa isu kara tobiori, daidokoro no doa ni mukaimashita.

Yoko was disappointed.

陽子はがっかりしました。

Yōko wa gakkari shimashita.

'Where are you going?' Yoko asked.

「どこへ行くの？」陽子は尋ねました。

'Doko e ikuno?' Yōko wa tazunemashita.

'To put the toothbrush away,' Chiharu replied.

「歯ブラシを片付けるの」と千春は答えました。

'Haburashi o katadzukeruno' to Chiharu wa kotaemashita.

'How then will you make a wish?' Chiharu stopped.

「じゃあ、どうやって願い事をするの？」と千春は
止まりました。

'Jā, dō yatte negaigoto o suru no?' to Chiharu wa tomarimashita.

Yoko went to check on the tempura frying on the
stove. It was perfect- light and fluffy. She took it off
and brought it to the table.

陽子はコンロで揚げている天ぷらを確認しに行きま
した。天ぷらは完璧に軽くてふわふわでした。陽子
はそれを取り、テーブルに持ってきました。

Yōko wa konro de ageteiru tempura o kakunin shi ni ikimashita.
Tempura wa kanpeki ni karukute fuwafuwadeshita. Yōko wa sore
o tori, tēburu ni motte kimashita

'There's one more thing,' she added.

「もう1つあるのよ。」と陽子は付け加えました。

`Mō hitotsu arunoyo' to Yōko wa tsukekuwaemashita.*

'You must make five wishes before the end of Obon, or your teeth might never grow back.'

「お盆が終わる前に五つの願いごとをしなければな
らないの。そうしないと、あなたの歯は元に戻らな
い」

Obon ga owaru mae ni itsutsu no negaigoto o shinakereba naranaino. Sōshinaito, anata no ha wa moto ni modoranai.

Chiharu gasped. She reached across the table for the tempura and dropped her chopsticks on the floor.

千春は息をのみました。テーブルの向こう側の天ぷら
を取ろうと手を伸ばし、箸を床に落としてしまいまし
た。

Chiharu wa iki o nomimashita. Tēburu no mukōgawa no tempura o torouto te o nobashi, hashi o yuka ni otoshiteshimaimashita.

'Oh no!'Chiharu cried.

「あぁ！」千春は叫びました。

Ā! Chiharu wa sakebimashida.

As she bent down to pick up the toothbrush she had a thought. She got back up.

千春は歯ブラシを拾うためにかがむと、ある考えが浮かびました。千春は起き上がりました。

Chiharu wa haburashi o hirou tame ni kagamuto, aru kangae ga ukabi mashita. Chiharu wa okiagarimashita.

'Please tell me how this toothbrush works.'

「この歯ブラシのしくみを教えて」

'Kono haburashi no shikumi o oshiete.'

It had been many years since Yoko had seen a magic toothbrush. She thought about it and remembered.

陽子が魔法の歯ブラシを見たのは何年も前のことです。陽子は考え、思い出しました。

Yōko ga mahō no haburashi o mita no wa nannen mo mae no kotodesu. Yōko wa kangae, omoidashimashita.

'There should be something written on the side of it.'

「横に何か書かれているはずよ」
'Yoko ni nanika kakarete iru hazuyo.'

Chiharu studied the toothbrush.

千春は歯ブラシを調べました。
Chiharu wa haburashi o shirabe mashita.

It read:

記し：
Shirushi:

MAGIC TOOTHBRUSH DO AS I SAY

魔法の歯ブラシ、 私の言う通り

Mahō no haburashi, watashi no iu tōri

TURN INTO [BLANK SPACE] RIGHT AWAY.

今すぐ[何か]に変わりなさい。

Imasugu [nanika] ni kawarinasai.

She flipped the toothbrush over and read the rest of the words.

千春は歯ブラシをひっくり返し、残りの言葉を読みました。

Chiharu wa haburashi o hikkurikaeshi, nokori no kotoba o yomimashita.

THANK YOU [BLANK SPACE] FOR HELPING ME TODAY, TURN BACK INTO A TOOTHBRUSH WITHOUT DELAY.

[何か]今日は私を助けてくれてありがとう、今すぐ歯ブラシに戻りなさい。

Kyō wa watashi o tasukete kurete arigatō, imasugu haburashi ni modorinasai.

Chiharu decided to make her first wish.

千春は最初の願い事をすることにました。

Chiharu wa saisho no negaigoto o suru koto ni shimashita.

'Magic toothbrush, do as I say, turn into chopsticks right away.'

「魔法の歯ブラシ、私の言う通り
今すぐお箸に変わりなさい」

Mahō no haburashi, watashi no iu tōri imasugu ohashini kawarinasai.

Immediately, the toothbrush turned into a pair of chopsticks.

歯ブラシはすぐに箸に変わりました。

Haburashi wa sugu ni hashi ni kawarimashita.

Chiharu   gasped.

千春は息をのみました。

Chiharu wa iki o nomimashita.

She fixed the chopsticks between her fingers and ate. When she finished, she jumped up ready for her journey to obaasan's house.

千春は箸を指で持ち食べ始めました。食べ終わった後、千春は立ち上がっておばあさんの家への旅行の準備をしました。

Chiharu wa hashi o yubi de mochi tabe hajimemashita. Tabeowatta ato, Chiharu wa tachiagatte obāsan no ie e no ryokō no junbi o shimashita.

'Chiharu, have you forgotten something?' Yoko asked.

「千春、何か忘れてるんじゃない？」陽子は尋ねました。

`Chiharu, nanika wasureterunjanai?' Yōko wa tazunemashita.

Chiharu reversed the spell.

千春は呪文を逆転させました。

Chiharu wa jumon o gyakuten sasemashita.

'Thank you, chopsticks, for helping me today. Turn back into a toothbrush without delay.'

「お箸さん、今日は私を助けてくれてありがとう。すぐに歯ブラシに戻りなさい」

`Ohashisan, kyō wa watashi o tasukete kurete arigatō.
Imasugu haburashi ni modorinasai.

At once, the chopsticks turned back into a toothbrush.

すぐに、箸は歯ブラシに戻りました。

Sugu ni hashi wa haburashi ni modorimashita.

Chiharu smiled. *This is going to be easy,* she thought to herself.

千春は微笑みました。歯ブラシを持っていると全て簡単にいくだろうと思いました。

Chiharu wa hohoemimashita. Haburashi o motte iru to subete kantan ni iku   darō   to   omotimashia.

CHAPTER 3
Thirst
渇き

Yoko and Chiharu got ready.

陽子と千春は徳島に行く準備をしました。

Yōko to Chiharu wa Tokushima ni iku junbi o shimashita.

On the way to obaasan's house, Chiharu thought about all the things she could wish for with the magic toothbrush. She had four more wishes left.

おばあさんの家に行く途中、千春は魔法の歯ブラシで何ができるかを考えていました。

願い事はあと四つ。

Obāsan no ie ni iku tochū, Chiharu wa mahō no haburashi de nani ga dekiru noka o kangaete imashita. Negaigoto wa ato yottsu.

They arrived in Tokushima in time for lunch. Obaasan had made them sweet rice cakes with red beans; it was Chiharu's favourite treat.

陽子と千春は昼食に間に合うように徳島に到着しました。おばあさんはおはぎを作っていました。千春の大好きなおやつです。

Yōko to Chiharu wa chūshoku ni maniau yō ni Tokushima ni tōchaku shimashita. Obāsan wa ohagi o tsukutteimashita. Chiharu no daisuki na oyatsudesu.

Chiharu told obaasan about the magic toothbrush.

千春はおばあさんに魔法の歯ブラシについて話しま
した。

Chiharu wa o bāsan ni mahō no haburashi ni tsuite hanashimashita.

'Use it wisely,' she advised.

「よく考えて使うといいわ」とおばあさんは忠告
しました。

'Yoku kangaete tsukauto iiwa.' to obāsan wa chūkoku shimashita.

After lunch, obaasan showed them around her garden. She took great care of it. She had a separate area for the fruits and vegetables. She was delighted with the new gardening tools Yoko had bought her.

昼食後、おばあさんは千春と陽子を庭に案内しまし
た。おばあさんが手入れしている大切な庭です。果
物と野菜を別々に育ててました。
おばあさんは陽子が買った新しい園芸工具に満足し
ていました。

Chūshokugo, o*bāsan* wa Chiharu to Yōko o niwa ni annai shimashita. O*bāsan* ga teire shiteiru taisetsu na niwa desu.
Kudamono to yasai o betsubetsuni sodatete imashita.
O*bāsan* wa Yōko ga katta atarashī engei kōgu ni manzoku shite imashita.

The heat in the garden became too much for Chiharu and made her thirsty. Rather than go indoors for a drink, she decided to make a second wish.

庭はとても暑く、千春は喉が渇いてきました。
千春は部屋に戻って飲み物を飲む代わりに、もう一度願い事をすることにしました。

Niwa wa totemo atsuku, Chiharu wa nodo ga kawaitekimashita. Chiharu wa heya ni modotte nomimono o nomu kawarini mōichido negaigoto o suru koto ni shimashita.

'Magic toothbrush, do as I say, turn into a glass of water right away. '

「魔法の歯ブラシ、私の言う通り、今すぐコップ一杯の水に変わりなさい」

'Mahō no haburashi, watashi no iu tōri
Imasugu koppuippai no mizu ni kawarinasai.'

Immediately, the toothbrush turned into a glass of water. Chiharu gulped it down in one go.

すぐに、歯ブラシはコップ一杯の水に変わりました。千春は一気にそれを飲みました。

Sugu ni, haburashi wa koppuippai no mizu ni kawarimashita. Chiharu wa ikkini sore o nomimashita.

When she reversed the spell, she became thirsty again. 'Oh no!' She sighed as she remembered Obaasan's words.

　千春が呪文を逆に言うと、また喉が渇いてしまいました。

あぁ！千春はおばあさんの言葉を思い出しながらため息をつきました。

Chiharu ga jumon o gyaku ni iuto, mata nodo ga kawaite shimaimashita.

Ā! Chiharu wa obāsan no kotoba o omoidashite tameiki o tsukimashita.

Chiharu sat on the steps upset.

千春は動揺して階段に腰を下ろしました。

Chiharu wa dōyō shite kaidan ni koshi o oroshimashita.

CHAPTER 4

The Secret's Out!

秘密がばれた！

It was the first day of Obon. Chiharu could hear laughter coming from the kitchen. She smiled and blew a kiss in the air. *It will be a good day* she thought to herself. She jumped out of bed and went to the kitchen.

お盆の初日でした。台所から笑い声が聞こえてきました。千春は微笑んで投げキッスをしました。今日はきっと良い日になるでしょう。千春はベッドから飛び降りて台所に行きました。

Obon no shonichideshita. Daidokoro kara waraigoe ga kikoetekimashita. Chiharu wa hohoende nage kissu o shimashita.

Kyō wa kitto yoi hi ni narudeshō. Chiharu wa beddo kara tobiorite daidokoro ni ikimashita.

'Ohayou,'
'Ohayou,' they said, greeting each other good morning.

「おはよう」 "Ohayō,"

「おはよう」 "Ohayō"

お互いに挨拶をしました。
Otagai ni aisatsu o shimashita.

Obaasan had made natto. Chiharu did not like natto, but she had kept this a secret between her and her father. She swirled her chopsticks around in her bowl.

おばあさんは納豆を作っていました。

千春が納豆を好きでないことは千春と亡くなったお父さんとの2人だけの秘密でした。

千春はお箸を茶碗の中でぐるぐると渦巻かせました。

obāsan wa nattō o tsukutte imashita. Chiharu ga nattō o sukidenaikoto wa, Chiharu to nakunatta otōsan to no futaridake no himitsudeshita. Chiharu wa hashi o chawan no nakade guruguru to uzumakase mashita.

Chiharu wanted otoosan to come into the kitchen and distract everyone by asking them to share their plans for the day. This would give Chiharu enough time to scoop her food into his bowl. But sadly, he wasn't here this year to do that.

千春は、おとうさんが台所に来て、その日の予定をみんなに聞きながら気をそらしてくれればいいのに、と思いました。そうすれば食べ物を取り皿に入れる時間ができるのに。

しかし悲しいことに、お父さんは今年ここにいません。

Chiharu wa otōsan ga *daidokoro ni kite sonohino yotei o minnani kikinagara ki o sorashite kurereba iinoni, to omoimashita. Sōsureba tabemono o torizara ni ireru jikan ga dekirunoni. Shikashi kanashii koto ni,* otōsan wa kotoshi kokoni imasen.

'Is anything the matter?' asked Yoko, pretending not to know about Chiharu's secret.

「何か問題でも？」千春の秘密を知らないふりをして陽子は尋ねました。

'Nanika mondai demo?'
Chiharu no himitsu o shiranaifuri o shite Yōko wa tazunemashita.

The secret was out. They laughed.
秘密がばれていたことに、みんなで笑いました。
Himitsu ga barete itakono ni, minnade wa waraimashita.

CHAPTER 5

Onsen

温泉

After breakfast, Yoko drove to a hot spring, it began to rain heavily.

朝食後、陽子は千春たちを連れて温泉に行きましたが、大雨が降りだしました。

Chōshokugo, Yōko wa Chiharutachi o tsurete onsen ni ikimashita ga, ōame ga furidashimashita.

They waited in the car park for the rain to stop, but it was continuous.

雨が止むことを期待して駐車場で待っていましたが、止むことはありませんでした。

Ame ga yamu koto o kitai shite chūshajō de matteimashita ga, yamukoto wa arimasen deshita.

Chiharu grew impatient and made a third wish.

ちはるは焦り、三回目のお願いをしました。

Chiharu wa aseri, sankaime no onegai o shimashita.

'Magic toothbrush, do as I say, turn into an umbrella right away. '

「魔法の歯ブラシ、私の言う通り、今すぐ傘に変わりなさい」

Mahō no haburashi, watahi no iu tōri, imasugu kasani kawarinasai.

Immediately, the toothbrush turned into an umbrella.

すぐに、歯ブラシは傘に変わりました。

Sugu ni, haburashi wa kasa ni kawarimashita.

They huddled up close together under the umbrella and made their way to the onsen. Chiharu placed the umbrella in the umbrella stand to dry, then went to get changed.

みんなで身を寄せ合って傘の中に入り温泉に向かい
ました。
千春は傘を乾かすために傘立てに入れ、更衣室に着
替えに行きました。

Minna de mi o yoseatte kasa no naka ni hairi onsen ni mukaimashita.
Chiharu wa kasa o kawakasutameni kasatateni ire, kōishitsu ni kigae ni
ikimashita.

The onsen was the perfect way to relax and spend time together. There were many baths inside. Chiharu liked the tub with bubbles.

温泉はリラックスして家族で一緒に過ごすのにぴっ
たりな方法でした。中にはたくさんのお風呂があり
ました。千春は泡風呂が気に入りました。

Onsen wa rirakkusu shite kazoku de sugosu no ni pittari na hōhō deshita.
Nakaniwa takusan no ofuro ga arimashita. Chiharu wa awaburo ga
kiniirimashita.

On the way home, Chiharu realized that she had forgotten something.

帰り道、千春は何かを忘れたことに気づきました。
Kaerimichi, Chiharu wa nanika o wasureta koto ni kidzukimashita.

'Wait!' she shouted.

"待って！"千春は叫びました。
" Matte!" Chiharu wa sakebi mashita.

She had forgotten to collect the umbrella from the umbrella stand. Yoko spun the car around and returned to the onsen.

千春は傘立てから傘を取るのを忘れしまったのです 。陽子は車を回して温泉に戻りました。

Chiharu wa kasatate kara kasa o toru no o wasurete shimattanodesu. Yōko wa kuruma o mawashite onsen ni modorimashita.

When they arrived at the onsen, there were many umbrellas in the stand.

温泉に到着すると、傘立てにはたくさんの傘があ りました。

Onsen ni tōchaku suruto, kasatate ni wa takusan no kasa ga arimashita.

Chiharu sighed. She took them out one by one and said the magic words each time.

千春はため息をつきました。傘を一つずつ取り出し 、その度に魔法の言葉を言いました。

Chiharu wa tameiki o tsukimashita. Kasa o hitotsuzutsu toridashi, sonotabi ni mahō no kotoba o iimashita.

'Thank you umbrella, for helping me today, turn back into a toothbrush without delay.'

「傘さん、今日は助けてくれてありがとう。すぐに歯ブラシに戻りなさい」

'Kasasan, kyōwa tasukete kurete arigatō. Sugu ni haburashi ni modorinasai.'

By the time she got to the last umbrella, she had lost all hope.

千春が最後の傘を手にしたとき、すべての希望を失い、がっかりました。

Chiharu ga saigo no kasa o te ni shita toki, subete no kibō o ushinai, gakkari shimashita.

She dropped her head and realised that her tooth might never grow back; just then, there was a clanking sound. The toothbrush was on the floor. She cried tears of joy.

千春は頭を落とし、歯が元に戻らないかもしれないことに気づきました。
ちょうどその時、カチッという音がしました。歯ブラシは床に落ちていました。千春は嬉し涙を流しました。

Chiharu wa atama o otoshi, ha ga motoni modoranai kamo shirenai koto ni kizukimashita. Chōdo sonotoki, kachitto iu oto ga shimashita. Haburashi wa yuka ni ochite imashita. Chiharu wa ureshinamida o nagashimashita.

They travelled home in silence.

千春たちは静かに家に帰りました。

Chiharutachi wa shizuka ni ie ni kaerimashita.

CHAPTER 6

Kōen

公園

After such an upsetting afternoon, Chiharu asked if she could go to the park.

そんな大変な事があった日の午後、千春は公園に行きたいと言いました。

Sonna taihenna koto ga atta hi no gogo, Chiharu wa kōen ni ikitai to iimashita.

Yoko told her to return by 6 o'clock.

陽子は6時までに戻るように言いました。

Yōko wa rokuji made ni modoru yō ni iimashita.

Chiharu hurried out the door.

千春は急いで玄関を出ました。

Chiharu wa isoide genkan o demashita.

Chiharu swung high on the swings and slid down the slides.

千春はブランコに乗って高くこぎ、すべり台をすべり降りました。

Chiharu wa buranko ni notte takaku kogi, suberidai o suberiorimashita.

She made a friend on the see-saw and said her goodbyes.

シーソーで友達を作り、さようならを言いました。

Shīsō de tomodachi o tsukuri, sayōnara o iimashita.

She joined another group of children by the climbing frame and gave up halfway on the monkey bars.

ジャングルジムで別の子供たちのグループに加わり、うんていの途中で諦めました。

Jangurujimu de betsu no kodomotachi no gurūpu ni kuwawari, untei no tochū de akiramemashita.

She tried again. She ran around, she stopped and ran around some more. Time passed by quickly.

千春はもう一度挑戦し、走り回り、少し立ち止まって、また走り回りました。

あっという間に時間が過ぎました。

Chiharu wa mouichido chōsenshi, hashirimawari, sukoshi tachidomatte, mata hashirimawari mashita.
Attoiumani jikan ga sugimashita.

She rolled up her sleeves to check the time, but she didn't have her watch on.

千春は時間を確認しようと袖をまくり上げました が、時計をつけていませんでした。

Chiharu wa jikan o kakunin siyō to sode o makuri agemashitaga, tokei o tsukete imasendeshita.

'Oh dear!' she cried.

「大変！」　千春は叫びました。

' Taihen ' Chiharu wa sakebi mashita.

Chiahru asked the children in the park for the time, but nobody could help her. It was getting late.

公園の子供たちに時間を尋ねました
が、誰も千春を助けることはできま
せんでした。だんだん日が暮れてき
ました。

Kōen no kodomotachi ni jikan o tazunemashitaga, dare mo Chiharu o tasukeru koto ga dekimasendeshita. Dandan higa kurete kimashita.

A thought came into her head. She reached for the toothbrush. 'Magic toothbrush, do as I say, turn into a watch right away.'

千春の頭に考えが思い浮かびました。

「魔法の歯ブラシ、私の言う通り、今すぐ腕時
計に変わりなさい」

Chiharu no atama ni kangae ga omoiukabimashita.
'Mahō no haburashi, watashino iutōri, imasugu udedokei ni kawarinasai.'

Immediately, the toothbrush turned into a watch, but it wasn't like her digital watch. She couldn't tell the time with this watch.

やがて歯ブラシは腕時計に変わりましたが、それは千春が持っていたようなデジタル腕時計ではありませんでした。千春は時間を読むことができませんでした。

Yagate haburashi wa udedokei ni kawarimashitaga, sore wa Chiharu ga motteita yōna dejitaru udedokei dewa arimasendeshita. Chiharu wa jikan o yomu koto ga dekimasen deshita.

A group of children sped past her on their bikes. She considered making another wish, but decided to run home instead.

子供たちのグループが自転車で千春を追い越しました。千春は別の願い事をしようと考えましたが、代わりに家に帰ることに決めました。

Kodomotachi no gurūpu ga jitensha de Chiharu o oikoshimashita. Chiharu wa betsu no negaigoto o shiyōto kangaemashitaga, kawarini ie ni kaeru koto ni kimemashita.

She reached home just in time and out of breath.

千春は時間通りに間に合い、息を切らせて家に着き
ました。

Chiharu wa jikan dōrini maniai, iki o kirasete ie ni tsukimashita.

Yoko was waiting for Chiharu outside the house.

陽子は家の外で千春を待っていました。

Yōko wa ie no soto de Chiharu o matteimashita.

'You left your watch in my bag.'

「腕時計を私の鞄に入れたままだったわよ」
`Udedokei o watashi no kaban ni ireta mama datta wayo.'

'I didn't want to get it wet, so I took it off at the hot spring... but I forgot to put it back on,' replied Chiharu.

「腕時計を濡らしたくなかったから温泉で外したんだけど、戻すのを忘れちゃった」と千春は答えました。
`Udedokei o nurashitakunakattakara onsen de hazushitandakedo, modosu no o wasurechatta.' to Chiharu wa kotaemashita.

'You are a smart girl,' Yoko replied.

「賢い子ね」と陽子は言いました。
`Kashikoi ko ne.' to Yōko wa iimashita.

'Don't forget it is obaasan's birthday tomorrow.'

「明日のおばあちゃんの誕生日、忘れないでね」
`Ashita no obāchan no tanjōbi, wasurenaide ne.'

Chiharu could see obaasan in the garden.

千春は庭のおばあさんが見えました。
Chiharu wa niwa no obāsan ga miemashita.

'What is obaasan doing?' she asked.

「おばあちゃんは何をしているの？」千春は尋ねました。
`Obāchan wa nani o shite iru no?' Chiharu wa tazunemashita.

She is picking flowers to take to ojiisan's grave.'

「おばあちゃんはおじいちゃんのお墓に飾る花を摘んでいるわ」

`Obāchan wa ojīchan no ohaka ni kazaru hana o tsunde iruwa.'

Chiharu thought about how she could celebrate obaasan's birthday. She went inside.

千春はおばあさんの誕生日をどうやって祝おうかと考えました。そして家に入りました。

Chiharu wa obāsan no tanjōbi o dō yatte iwaouka to kangaemashita. Soshite ie ni hairimasita.

In the evening, they took a stroll to the cemetery.

夕方、彼らは墓地まで散歩しました。

Yūgata, karera wa bochi made sanpo shimashita.

Obaasan laid down the flowers and cleaned his stone. Chiharu missed her grandfather very much. She remembered the long walks they had and the pictures he took of nature. She enjoyed those moments.

おばあさんは花を置き、お墓を片付けました。千春はおじいさんをとても恋しく思いました。一緒に歩いた長い散歩道、おじいさんが撮った自然の写真を思い出しました。
千春はそんな時間が楽しかったのです。

Obāsan wa hana o oki, ohaka o katazukemashita. Chiharu wa ojīsan o totemo koushiku omoimashita. Isshoni aruita nagai sanpomichi, ojīsan ga totta shizen no shashin o omoidashimashita. Chiharu wa sonna jikan ga tanoshikattanodesu.

'Let's climb the mountain tomorrow,' Chiharu asked.

「明日は山に登ろう」と千春は尋ねました。

"Ashita wa yama ni noborou.' to Chiharu wa tazunemashita.

'My knees are tired,' obaasan replied.

「ひざが疲れているのよ」とおばあさんは答えました。

'Hiza ga tsukarete irunoyo.' to obāsan wa kotaemashita.

Chiharu begged. They agreed to climb the next day.

千春は一生懸命お願いしました。
彼らは次の日、山に登ることに賛成しました。
Chiharu wa isshōkemmei onegai shimashita.
Karera wa tsuginohi, yamani noboru koto ni sansei shimashita.

CHAPTER 7

Enjoy The Moment

今を楽しむ！

It was an unusually windy day. Chiharu, Yoko, and Grandma were determined to climb to the top of the mountain, but it took a little longer.

それはいつになく風の強い日でした。千春、陽子、おばあさんは頂上に登ることを決意しましたが、山頂まではいつもより時間がかかりました。

Sore wa Itsuninaku tsuyoi kaze no hideshita. Chiharu, Yōko, obāsan wa chōjō ni noboru koto o ketsui shimashitaga, sanchō made wa itsumoyori jikan ga kakarimasita.

Chiharu remembered climbing the mountain with otoosan and ojiisan.

千春はお父さんとおじいさんと一緒に山に登ったことを思い出しました。

Chiharu wa otōsan to ojīsan to issho ni yama ni nobotta koto o omoidashimashita.

It brought back happy and sad memories.

それは幸せで悲しい思い出を呼び戻しました。

Sore wa shiawasede kanashī omoide o yobimodoshimashita.

'Try to enjoy the journey; it's better than the endpoint,' otoosan would say. Chiharu began to understand what he meant. She slowed down and waited for Yoko and obaasan.

「旅路は目的地に到着する事よりも楽しいんだよ」とお父さんは言うでしょう。千春はお父さんが何を意味していたのか理解し始めました。千春は減速し、陽子とおばあさんを待ちました。

`Tabiji wa mokutekichi ni tōchaku surukoto yori mo tanoshī ndayo.' to Otōsan wa iudeshō. Chiharu wa Otōsan ga nani o imi shiteita no ka rikai shihajimemashita. Chiharu wa gensoku shi, Yōko to Obāsan o machimashita.

When they reached the top of the mountain, they praised each other for their efforts.

頂上に着いたとき、千春たちはお互いの努力を褒め合いました。

Chōjō ni tsuita toki, Chiharu tachi wa otagai no doryoku o homeaimashita.

'Look here!' Chiharu called.

"ここを見て！"千春は叫びました。

" Koko o mite!" Chiharu wa sakebimashita.

She had found the place where otoosan used to stop for a drink. It had the most fantastic view of Tokushima.

千春はお父さんが飲み物のために立ち寄っていた場所を見つけました。
そこでは徳島で一番素晴らしい景色を眺める事ができました。

Chiharu wa Otōsan ga nomimono no tameni tachiyoteita basho o mitsukemashita.
Sokode wa Tokushima de ichiban subarashī keshiki o nagamerukotoga dekimashita.

'Let's take a picture of the family,' Chiharu suggested.

'That's a great idea, but no one has brought a camera,' Yoko replied.

「家族写真を撮ろうよ」と千春は提案しました。

「それは素晴らしい考えね、でも誰もカメラを持ってきていないの」と陽子は答えました。

'Kazoku shashin o torō yo.' to Chiharu wa teian shimashita.
'Sore wa subarashī kangae ne, demo daremo kamera o mottekiteinaino.' to Yōko wa kotaemashita.

'I will make my final wish then,' Chiharu decided.

「わたし、最後のお願いをするわ」と千春は決心しました。

'Watashi, saigo no onegai o suruwa' to Chiharu wa kesshin shimashita.

'Are you sure? 'Yoko asked.

「本当に？」陽子は尋ねました。

.'Hontōni? ' Yōko wa tazunemashita.

'Yes, I'm sure. '

「うん。本当よ」
' Un. Hontōyo. '

'Magic toothbrush, do as I say, turn into a camera right away.'

「魔法の歯ブラシ、私の言う通り、今すぐカメラに変わりなさい」
'Mahō no haburashi, watashi no iu tōri, imasugu kamera ni kawarinasai.'

Immediately, the toothbrush changed into a camera, but it was a Polaroid camera. This was not what Chiharu expected.

歯ブラシはすぐにカメラに変わりましたが、それはポラロイドカメラでした。それは千春が期待したものではありませんでした。

Haburashi wa sugu ni kamera ni kawarimashitaga, sorewa poraroidokamera deshita. Sore wa Chiharu ga kitai shita monode wa arimasendeshita.

She shrugged and asked a passerby to take a family photograph of them.

千春は肩をすくめて通行人に家族写真を撮ってもらいました。

Chiharu wa kata o sukumete tsūkōnin ni kazoku shashin o totte moraimashita.

An instant film ejected from the camera.

カメラからインスタントフィルムが出てきました。

Kamera kara insutantofirumu ga detekimashita.

Chiharu remembered the film that use to eject from ojiisan's camera. She shook it from side to side as he used to do.

千春はおじいさんのカメラから飛び出したインスタントフィルムを思い出しました。

おじいさんが以前やっていたようにそれを左右に振りました。

Chiharu wa ojīsan no kamera kara tobidashita insutantofirumu o omoidashimashita. Ojīsan ga izen yatteitayōni sore o sayū ni furimashita.

The wind blew the film out of her hand, and landed on a drinks machine. She ran to peel it off.

その時風が吹き、千春の手からフィルムを吹き飛ばし、自動販売機機械の前に落ちました。千春は駆け寄ってフィルムを取りました。

Sonotoki toppū ga fuki, Chiharu no te kara firumu o fukitobashimashi, jidōhanbaiki no mae ni ochimashita. Chiharu wa kakeyotte firumu o torimashita.

She stared in a daze at the bottles of water in the machine.

千春は自動販売機の中の水のボトルをぼんやりと見つめていました。

Chiharu wa jidōhanbaiki no naka no mizu no botoru o bonyari to mitsumete imashita.

She remembered what had happened in obaasan's garden with the glass of water.

千春はおばあさんの庭でコップ一杯の水に何が起こったのかを思い出しました。

Chiharu wa o bāsan no niwa de koppuippai no mizu ni nani ga okotta no ka o omoidashimashita.

She then thought about what might happen when she reversed the spell. She sighed. What if the photograph disappeared like the glass of water did.

千春は、呪文を逆にするとカメラのフィルムはどう なるのだろうと思いました。千春はため息をつきま した。

写真がコップ一杯の水のように消えてしまったら？

Chiharu wa, jumon o gyaku ni suruto kamera no firumu wa dō naru nodarou to omoimashita. Chiharu wa tameiki o tsukimashita. Shashin ga koppuippai no mizu no yō ni kieteshimattara?

At this point, Chiharu did not care about her tooth growing back; she just didn't want to lose the memory of the photograph. Obaasan and Yoko comforted her. 'Don't worry. It will all be okay,' they said.

しかしこの時、千春は自分の歯が戻らなくなる事よ りも、この写真の思い出を失いたくないと思ってい ました。

おばあさんと陽子は千春をなぐさめました。

「心配ないわ。大丈夫よ。」

Shikashi konotoki, Chiharu wa jibunno ha ga modoranakunarukoto yorimo, kono shashin no omoide o ushinaitakunai to omotte imashita.

Obāsan to *Yōko wa Chiharu o nagusamemashita.*

`Shinpainaiwa. Daijōbu yo.'

Yoko put the camera in her bag and took out the birthday card that Chiharu had made for obaasan. She wished her a happy birthday but her heart was broken.

陽子はカメラを鞄に入れ、千春がおばあさんのために作った誕生日カードを取り出しました。千春はお誕生日おめでとうと言いましたが、心の中は失望していました。

Yōko wa kamera o kaban ni ire, Chiharu ga Obāsan no tame ni tsukutta tanjōbikādo o toridashimashita. Chiharu wa otanjōbi omedetō to ī mashitaga, kokorono nakawa shitsubō shiteimashita.

They took the ropeway back down the mountain.

彼らはロープウェイで山を下りました。

Karera wa rōpūwei de yama o orimashita.

When they arrived home, Obaasan put the photograph inside the card and put it in the cabinet along with the camera.

'It's almost time for bed now, why don't you go and have your bath.'

家に着くと、おばあさんは写真をカードの中に入れ、カメラと一緒に戸棚にしまいました。

「もうそろそろ寝る時間だよ。お風呂に入ろうか」

Ie ni tsuku to, obāsan wa shashin o kādo no naka ni ire, kamera to issho ni todana ni shimai mashita.

'Sorosoro nerujikandayo. Ofuro ni hairōka.'

Chiharu cried in the bath. She thought about everything that happened in the last few days.

千春はお風呂で泣きました。彼女は過去数日間に起こったことすべてについて考えました。

Chiharu wa ofuro de nakimashita. Chiharu wa kako sūjitsukan ni okotta koto subete ni tsuite kangaemashita.

She returned to her room and stared out the window.

千春は自分の部屋に戻り、窓の外を見つめました。

Chiharu wa jibun no heya ni modori, mado no soto o mitsumemashita.

She could see people going to the Awa Odori. She could hear the drums and bells. There was a knock on the door; it was Yoko wearing a yukata.

阿波おどりに行く人々が見えました。太鼓と鐘の音も聞こえてきました。
ドアがノックされました。それは浴衣を着た陽子でした。

Awa odori ni iku hitobito ga miemashita. Taiko to kane no oto mo kikoete kimashita.
Doa ga nokku saremashita. Sorewa yukata o kita Yōko deshita.

Yoko placed a yukata for Chiharu on the bed.

陽子は千春の浴衣をベッドに置きました。
Yōko wa Chiharu no yukata o beddo ni okimashita.

'Let's go to the Awa Odori,' Yoko said.

「阿波おどりに行こう」と陽子は言いました。
`Awa odori ni ikō.' to Yōko wa iimashita.

Obaasan entered the room also wearing a yukata. It was new. Chiharu smiled. She realized that it was a gift from Yoko.

おばあさんも浴衣を着て部屋に入ってきました。
浴衣は新品でした。千春は微笑みました。それはお
母さんからの贈り物だと気づいたのです。

Obāsan mo yukata o kite heya ni haitte kimashita. Yukata wa shinpindeshita.

Chiharu wa hohoenmimashita. Sore wa okāsan kara no okurimonodato kidzuitanodesu.

Awa Odori was as great as Yoko remembered. They danced with the rens and ate street food. They sat down and saw a great performance. That night, Chiharu went to be with her heart full.

阿波おどりは陽子の思い出通り、素晴らしいものでした。千春たちは連と踊り、屋台の食べ物を食べました。座って素晴らしい演技を見ました。
　その夜、千春は幸せな気持ちで眠りました。

Awa odori wa Yōko no omoide dōri, subarashī monodeshita. Chiharu tachi wa ren to odori, yatai no tabemono o tabemashita.

Suwatte subarashī engi o mimashita.

Sonoyoru, Chiharu wa shiawase na kimoshi de nemurimashita.

CHAPTER 8

The Moment Of Truth
真実の瞬間

The following morning, Chiharu woke to the buzzing of cicadas. Her heart sank as she remembered the camera. She went straight to the living room.

次の日の朝、千春は蝉の鳴き声で目が覚めました。
千春はカメラを思い出し、心が沈みました。千春はリ
ビングに直行しました。

Tsugino hi no asa, Chiharu wa semi no nakigoe de me ga samemashita. Chiharu wa kamera o omoidashi, kokoro ga shizunda. Chiharu wa ribingu ni chokkō shimashita.

The card was still in the glass cupboard, but there was no camera. Obaasan opened the cabinet and took out the card. The photo fell on the floor. It was blank.

カードはまだガラスの戸棚にありましたが、カメ
ラはありませんでした。
おばあさんはキャビネットを開けてカードを取り
出しました。
写真が床に落ちました。それは真っ白でし
た。

Kādo wa mada garasu no todana ni arimashitaga, kamera wa arimasendeshita. Obaāsan wa kyabinetto o akete kādo o toridashimashita. Shashin ga yuka ni ochimashita. Sore wa masshirodeshita.

Yōko picked it up and turned it over.

陽子はそれを手に取りひっくり返しました。

Yōko wa sore o teni tori hikkurikaeshimashita.

They sighed. Before them was the image at the top of the mountain.

彼らはため息をつき、山の頂上の画像を見て驚きました。

Karera wa tameiki o tsuki, yama no chōjō no gazō o mite odoroikimashita.

In the picture, there appeared to be two men that looked like otoosan and ojiisan but they couldn't be sure.

写真には、お父さんとおじいさんのように見える2人の男性が写っていましたが、そんな事が考えられるなんて不可能でした。

Shashin ni wa, otōsan to ojīsan no yōni mieru futari no dansei ga utsutte imashitaga, sonna kotoga kangaerareru nante fukanōdeshita.

Obaasan stood by the car to say her goodbyes. She turned to Chiharu.

おばあさんは車のそばに立ってさよならを言いました。そして千春の方に目を向けました。

Obāsan wa kuruma no soba ni tatte sayonara o iimashita. Soshite Chiharu no hōni me o mukemashita.

'I am very proud of you. Your mom and I weren't as smart as you when we were your age.'
She turned to Yoko and winked.

「私はあなたをとても誇りに思っているわ。あなたのお母さんと私があなたの年齢だったとき、あなたほど頭が良くなかったわ。 」

おばあさんは陽子の方を向いてウインクをしました。

`Watashi wa anata o totemo hokori ni omotte iruwa. Anata no okāsan to watashi ga anata no nenreidatta toki, anata hodo atama ga yoku nakattawa. `

Obāsan□wa Yōko□no hō o muite
winku o shimashita.

On the way back to Nagoya, Chiharu thought about everything that happened over the past few days.

名古屋に帰る途中、千春はここ数日間で起こったことについてもう一度考えました。

Nagoya ni kaeru tochū, Chiharu wa koko sūjitsukan de okotta kotoni tsuite mōichido kangaemashita .

Her magic toothbrush had gone, but she was pleased that the spirits of the past allowed her to make some of the most important decisions of her life.

千春の魔法の歯ブラシはもうなくなりましたが、過去の精霊が千春の人生で最も重要な決断のいくつかを彼女に託してくれた事を嬉しく思いました。

Chiharu no mahō no haburashi wa mō nakunarimashitaga, kako no seirei ga Chiharu no jinsei de mottomo jūyōna ketsudan no ikutsu ka o kanojoni takushitekuretakoto o ureshiku omoimashita.

This was one Obon, Chiharu would never forget.

このお盆の出来事を、千春は決して忘れないでしょう。

Kono obon no dekigoto o, Chiharu wa kesshite wasurenaideshō.

The end
終わり

Owari

BACKGROUND

I left London for Japan in 2011 to work as an English conversation teacher. This was the same year that Japan had experienced the Fukushima Daiichi nuclear disaster. Not everyone understood my reasons for wanting to go. However, I had made up my mind. The optimism I had built up slowly evaporated as I sat waiting at Nagoya Chubu Airport for the company director to pick me up. We'd discussed my flight details over email, so why hadn't he come to get me- *had I been duped.* My fears began to fade, following a phone call to head office. They confirmed that someone was indeed on their way to get me. That evening, as I lay my jet-lagged body on a futon mattress, on the hard floor, I questioned my migratory decision, whilst listening to overzealous twenty-something-year-olds ramble on about being in Japan. It comforted me to know that I was in Nagoya for just a few days to train as a Native teacher.

As I stood outside Tokushima station for the first time, the realisation hit me that this was going to be home for at least a year. I was already drawing comparisons to my hometown Brixton. The station was close by and the art was warm and welcoming.

Outside Tokushima station, Japan

Stockwell Park Walk (Brixton) London

Once in Tokushima, I was assigned to three schools in Yoshinogawa, Komatsushima and Matsushige.

I drew inspiration for this book from several sources and experiences. After finishing work at Matsushige, I would pass a billboard that showed a young girl flying on a toothbrush, *how wonderfully bizarre* I thought to myself, but so were a lot of things in Japan, such as the ability to grab a canned hot chocolate or tea from a vending machine.

The main character in this story is called Chiharu. There is no particular reason why I chose this name, other than that I taught two students with the same name. It's a beautiful sounding Japanese name, and its three syllables make it that more impactful. I wanted it to be apparent whenever someone picked up this book that we were going on a journey to Japan.

A part of teaching that I later came to appreciate was in my lessons with the older students. In these lessons, the students would be given a short extract about traditional festivals and holidays - such as Hinamatsuri, Setsuban, and Obon. What I gained from this, was a basic understanding of festivals and the culture, what's more, I was able to participate and experience these events for myself.

I was incredibly blessed to meet some phenomenal people whilst living in Japan. Through them, I was afforded an authentic Japanese experience. I joined Tokushima Christian Reformed Church and was involved in their children's ministry - Happy Kids. The Terauchi family were a God-send, and Miwa Numata-san always made sure that whenever there was an opportunity to experience something *Japanesy* (as I would say), I would be part of it. Through her, I met Kimiko Matsumura-san, a wonderful garden designer, incredibly knowledgeable in her field; the garden scene in the story was a nod to her.

I took on a casual job at T Place, a talking café, where I sat and talked with local Japanese visitors about every and anything - mostly current affairs. Thank you Tony Masuya-san for having the vision to set up such an inclusive establishment where one can learn from and about each other. There I met the merry Kelekolio Maka- san his wife Mary Maka-san and their wonderful children. I met Yoko-san (respectfully) an unassuming warm-hearted lady with a heart of gold. We had many memorable conversations whilst dining at either a quaint, Eurocentric, or traditional restaurant in Tokushima. Sadly, we lost contact, but I often get a sense of natsukashi (nostalgia) when I revisit my photographs.

Another blessing came in the form of the Fushitani family. I built a wonderful friendship with Kana-san, her husband Akira-san and children Yuka and Ryotaro Fushitani. I always felt like part of the family. The experiences we shared were invaluable, and Kana-san's aura was always so peaceful and contented.

No gaijin (foreigner) could live in Tokushima without visiting Bourbon Street Music Bar, a mellow jazz place. One could always expect a warm welcome from Vivian Hernaez-san, and for those with a bit more verve – the place to be was Ingrid's Bar for a tad of karaoke and dancing till the early hours. Ingrid Hashimoto-san has touched so many different lives.

I worked along with some fantastic and committed teachers in Tokushima - Kana Thomason-san, whose enthusiasm and energy for teaching was unmatched.

One of my biggest regrets about living in Japan was not being wholly present in the moment. There are elements of this embedded in the story.

Being present is a work in progress, the here and now is the greatest gift. If I never speak of Japan again - I am content knowing that I've finally published this book.

OTHER BOOKS BY JOANA JEHU APPIAH:

Elijah: Journeying Through a Pandemic

Akwasi Has Arrived